TaiLorMade Books Presents

We Were Still Kids

By Nataisha T. Hill

May not be suitable for children under the age of 16

Chapter 1

"Wake up, Charlie!" Her grandmother would scream through the short hallway of their small two-bedroom home in the back woods. Grandma Rose was old school. She planted her own garden, hand washed her own clothes, and slopped hogs in the backyard pin. Charlie would pretend not to hear her, not only because she hated getting up in the morning, but she also hated school. Her older sister and younger brother, on the other hand, made a mark on their classmates with his charming personality and her sister's stunning looks. Charlie was the average eleven-year-old, tall but not too tall, skinny, with fair brown skin and beautiful curly hair. She had a cute face until she stood next to her thirteen-year-old sister's long, flowing hair, beautiful caramel skin, and perfect white teeth.

She always felt that her grandmother knew her sister was prettier, since Grandma would teach Charlie all her outdoor skills while Jodie stayed in the house cooking and cleaning.

They all slept in the same room on a huge bed with one box spring and three mattresses stacked on top of one another. Joseph, her younger brother who they called Joey, and Jodie, the oldest, instantly got up in the mornings, but Charlie always dragged behind. She loved when grandma would call her out aside from them. It made her feel special in a way. Grandma Rose made her feel that it was important that her presence existed at the table. Who was Charlie kidding? The smell of fried chicken and apples at 5:30am sent her senses into overdrive. She had no choice but to get up.

"Now Charlie, I done told you to stop procrastinating like a Gisabelle on her wedding day," Grandma would say, as they would all laugh. They never really knew what it meant.

Joseph, who was only eight years old, would pour Charlie's juice and set it on the table in front if the chair right next to him. Their bond was special. Charlie always looked out for little Joey and would beat up any kid who messed with him. The children had to hide their fights from grandma because she would have their hind parts if she knew Charlie was fighting Joey's battles.

Charlie figured that Joey had concluded that Jodie was too pretty to fight because he never told Jodie when he was being bullied. Besides, Charlie kind of thought grandma wanted her to take up for Joey since Charlie felt like Joey was Grandma's favorite. There was a little envy when it came to Joey because he never had to do any of the chores that the girls did. He would look at Grandma with those brown eyes and say, 'I just love u grandma' every time they sat down at the table.

Every morning grandma would tell them the same story about an old man in a hat. She said to never go near the old man on the corner with the brown hat because he always had bad tricks under it. They would all snicker, not knowing what it meant. Then, she would quiz them on scriptures they were supposed to read after they had finished their homework the previous night.

"Who got caught in that den with those lions?"

"David did, Grandma Rose," answered Joey with chicken in his mouth.

"Who did Abraham offer as a sacrifice?"

"Abraham sacrificed his own son, Grandma."

"That's right. And what was his name, baby?"

"His name was Isaac, Grandma."

She would look at Charlie and give her a small grin of approval as if she already knew that Charlie had already told Joey all the answers. Grandma never really spoke about their parents. Charlie was around three when their parents left and Jodie said she couldn't remember much. However, Jodie said that she did remember their mom being super gorgeous.

Grandma Rose would tell them however that their mom loved them dearly and she had to go away for a while. They would ask their grandma, 'What's a while and when were they coming back?' She'd respond by saying, 'Why? Do y'all want to leave me here alone to die?' They eventually learned to stop asking grandma about their parents returning.

After breakfast they would walk up what seemed like a never-ending driveway to get on the bus each morning. The kids on their bus were just as poor as them, so they had no problems with them. In fact, their entire neighborhood was consistent with old school traditions except for a few kids having washers and dryers. It was the early 80's, they didn't know anything different besides what they had seen on the one black-and-white television that grandma had in the front room.

They all separated once they got to school. Charlie made sure Joey got to his class and who knows where Jodie went. She had caught Jodie skipping class on several occasions, but she never told grandma. On her way to class, Charlie thought about how much she hated her teacher. She was fat, mean, and Charlie didn't think she liked kids.

She walked into her classroom with no intentions of listening or learning until she met Mr. Frye. Mr. Frye was a tall black man with a stern face. He wore his glasses on his nose as he walked into the room with a brown hat and a brown trench coat. Instantly, her grandmother's early morning saying about the man on the corner echoed in her mind, but she figured Mr. Frye was okay since they weren't on the corner.

He explained that Mrs. Kindle had family issues and he would be the temporary substitute teacher for the next few months. He told them funny jokes about animals and old people. He had the entire class bursting into laughter. He was some character, so Charlie knew it would be the best year ever. She just hoped that Mrs. Kindle would be gone forever instead of just temporarily.

When class was over, Charlie stayed behind because she had a few questions to ask Mr. Frye.

"Uh…Mr. Frye," she began, "I wanted to know is our teacher really gone for the rest of the year?"

"Why? Do you want her to be gone?" He curiously responded.

"Well, Mr. Frye, you see sir…yes Mr. Frye, I want her gone."

"That's not a nice thing to say."

"It's just that I don't think she liked me, sir."

"Why do you say that, Charlie? Your name is little Charlie, right?"

"Well, just Charlie, sir. She always gave me funny looks and write-offs when it wasn't my fault, Mr. Frye."

"Well, maybe she just wanted to make you laugh and she enjoyed your handwriting," he said and snickered.

"Yeah Mr. Frye, I think things just may work out."

"You look familiar, Charlie, what's your mom's name?"

"Miss Joanna, sir."

"Miss Joanna?" he said, as he started thinking aloud.

Charlie quickly began to pack her backpack. She didn't want Mr. Frye asking questions that she couldn't answer, so she told him she had to go. Charlie then noticed Jodie trying to get her attention from the side of the classroom door. She couldn't understand what Jodie was whispering, so she walked closer to the door.

"Hey Charlie, Joey is in in-school suspension again and I need you to get him out," Jodie said, moving back toward the hallway when she saw Mr. Frye.

"Well, look at here. Who might you be?" asked Mr. Frye.

"Oh, my name is Jodie, Charlie's older sister. Come on, Charlie!" Jodie impatiently said, dragging Charlie by the arm.

"Now wait a minute, Ms. Jodie, I just may have to put you in my after-school detention for disrupting my class."

"Uh, yeah, but your class is over, sir," said Jodie, looking confused.

"Are you trying to rebel against authority, miss?"

"No, Mr. Frye, you don't understand, we have to...-"

"Thank you for the talk, Mr. Frye," said Charlie, rushing out the room, grabbing Jodie's arm.

"What's his problem?" Jodie asked as they continued to rush to Joey's rescue.

"Nothing, he's just a new teacher. He's trying to fit in, I guess."

Charlie didn't want to admit to Jodie that she didn't want her to reveal that they lived with their grandmother. Charlie figured it would have only led to more questions about their mother.

"Anyhow, why is my little Joey in detention?" Charlie asked.

"Some girl was picking on him, so he poured milk all down the front of her pants."

"Wow...that's my Joey."

Once they arrived at the detention room, the principal set at the desk opposed to the normal detention teacher. Principal Fields was one of the meanest men that Charlie had ever met. There was no way he was going to agree to allow Joey to go home.

"Oh no, what do we do now, Jodie?"

Chapter 2

"I got you covered this time, girls," a voice said from behind. The girls turned around only to see the one and only Mr. Frye, walking up from behind them. *What did he mean he had them covered?* Charlie wondered. *What was he going to do?*

"Mr. Fields," he firmly said as he walked over to shake the principal's hand. "I actually came for the boy, Joseph, sir. These children owe me some board cleaning and I wanted to get them on the bus in time, so their parents wouldn't worry."

"Little Joey, you're in luck, Mr. Frye just saved your little hind parts, boy," whispered Jodie to Joey.

A sigh of relief came over Charlie. Normally, when you had detention at the end of the day, they called the parents to come get the students. Lord forbid if grandma had to be called from the sawmill factory. She would have had all their hinds.

It wasn't a secret. They lived in a predominately black community. Everyone knew that if the school reported any mischief to parents, the next day they called you R&R, which meant raw rear. The kids were silent as they walked down the hall with Mr. Frye. They weren't sure what he was going to do. They weren't sure if he was going to tell their grandmother anyway. They didn't say a thing as they loaded up in his 1971 brown Chevy classic.

Jodie sat in the front and gave Mr. Frye directions to their home. As calm as Jodie seemed, Charlie was still petrified that grandma would see a teacher dropping them off. Even though he was Charlie's teacher, to grandma, he was a stranger. There was nothing worse to grandma than to see her kids with a stranger. Their grandma normally didn't get home until about an hour after they did, but Charlie didn't want any surprises and her neighbors were very nosey.

"Mr. Frye, sir, could you drop us off around the corner? Grandma Rose wouldn't be pleased if she saw a grown man taking us home," Charlie explained.

Mr. Frye looked at Charlie through his mirror but didn't say anything. He glanced at Jodie who nodded her head in approval. He pulled over by an abandoned house a few blocks away and turned off the car.

"Well kids, I wanted you to know that Mr. Frye is good at keeping secrets, too. I live a few blocks down from here off Scottville Road. I want you kids to come rake some leaves for me and earn some afterschool money."

"Money!" They all said in unison.

"Yeah, money," he repeated and laughed. "Haven't you kids had after school jobs before?"

"No, sir. We normally have to do the chores around grandma's house. We don't get paid for those. Like grandma always says, she provides the food, clothing, and shelter, so we should be grateful just for that," Charlie responded.

Mr. Frye laughed. "She's right, but since you don't live with me, I will offer you some compensation. Also, if you would like to keep a little to the side for yourself, I will tell your grandmother that I am only giving you half of what I actually give you."

Charlie didn't know how to respond. Why would he be under the impression that their grandma would take their money? Yes, they were a little on the poor side, but grandma wouldn't take something they rightfully earned. Would she? Besides, Charlie didn't feel comfortable lying to grandma. She knew what would happen if grandma found out about the lie. However, this was different. She wouldn't be the one lying to grandma, Mr. Frye was.

"I guess that's okay. We would have to ask grandma first, but I guess it's okay," Charlie repeated, not sure how grandma would respond.

"That's fine with me. Hey, I need you two to do me a big favor."

"Anything for you, Mr. Frye," Joey responded as if he was talking to his new best friend.

"I need you two to stand outside for a few seconds. I want to ask your sister some mature questions since she is the oldest."

Joey and Charlie happily got out of the car, feeling as if that day was their lucky day. They were going to start making money as kids. They would be the most popular kids in their neighborhood.

Moments later, Jodie got out of the car with a weary look on her face. They waited until Mr. Frye pulled off before bombarding her with questions. Jodie acted as if she was in a trance. She didn't move as she watched his car until it disappeared out of sight.

"What's wrong, Jodie? Did he say he changed his mind?" Joey asked.

"No." She said, still looking off in the distance.

"Did he say he was going to tell grandma?" Joey continued to question.

"No, Joey," she said, now storming off.

"Well, wait Jodie, what is it?" Charlie asked.

"I don't know if I should tell you." Jodie began. "You can't be upset in front of grandma. She'll smell that something is wrong. Besides, it may be too much for you two to handle."

"No, it isn't, tell us," demanded Charlie.

They begged her even more as they got closer to home. Their begging seemed to have cheered her up as she laughed while they both pulled her arms. They started dancing around her in circles.

"Okay, okay…pickle heads, but you have to keep it a secret. You can't tell anyone. Don't even tell yourselves again."

"Come on, Jodie, tell us," whined Joey.

"Mr. Frye said he knows our mother and he knows where we can find her."

Chapter 3

Charlie and Joey stood stiff as they looked at Jodie in awe. Joey was young enough to go for it, but Charlie was skeptical. She couldn't believe that Jodie was falling for it, too.

"He's a liar. How would he know our parents?" Charlie asked.

"Well, he asked me who did we stay with, and when I told him Grandma Rose, he said 'yeah, I know your parents. Y'all are those Johnson kids' and I hadn't told him anything," Jodie explained.

"Well, duh, that's my teacher, so I'm sure it wouldn't be hard for him to remember my last name," Charlie said in a matter-of-fact tone.

"Everybody knows he's just a temporary replacement for Ms. Kindle," teased Jodie.

"So?"

"So…what makes you think you're so special that he learned your last name in one day?"

"At least I don't believe everything I hear. You're more gullible than Joey and he's the youngest."

"And you're just mad he told me about mom and not you because he thinks I'm the pretty one," Jodie snapped back.

"Yeah, pretty ugly," Joey said, playfully pushing Jodie's arm and running towards the porch.

As Jodie ran after him towards the house, Charlie's feelings were hurt. Not because of what Jodie said about their looks; Charlie already knew Jodie was prettier than her. Charlie just didn't think that Mr. Frye would like Jodie more than he liked her.

About an hour or so later grandma had arrived home from work. Charlie was sitting in the front room sulking. She tried to hide her feelings, but she clearly wasn't good at it.

"Pick your face up, girl, before somebody step on it," said Grandma Rose as she walked toward the kitchen.

"Yes, grandma," she softly replied.

"What's the matter with you, Charlie?"

Charlie knew she couldn't hide anything from her grandma, but she didn't want to tell her what was bothering her. Charlie figured she'd whip her butt if she told her grandmother she was sad over something silly such as not being favored by a teacher.

"Everything was going fine until I got to homeroom this morning. We got a new teacher, grandma, and I'm not sure if things will work out," she finally said.

"Oh, it'll be okay, Charlie, I'm sure your teacher will like you just as much as the old teacher did. Now, go wash up for dinner."

"Ok, grandma."

Later that evening, Charlie quietly sat down at the dinner table and kept her mouth full, so she didn't have to do a lot of talking. Grandma told the others Charlie was upset because her old teacher was gone, but Jodie knew better. She knew she had crossed the line. Charlie could tell Jodie felt bad from the way she put her head down every time Charlie looked across the table at her.

After dinner, grandma made them clean up and get ready for bed. Joey had to get his hair brushed every night, so his eczema wouldn't flare up on his scalp. This gave Jodie a little time to talk to Charlie alone. She gave Charlie a push as they hopped in the bed.

"Are u still mad at me?" Jodie asked.

"No, who could stay mad at the prettiest girl in the world."

"Come on, really, Charlie? I didn't mean anything by it, besides; you are my sister, so you look just like me."

"I'm flattered," Charlie said, forging a fake smile.

"Come on, are we cool again, or do I have to call u a pretty toad for the rest of the week?"

They both started to laugh. They laughed so hard that grandma yelled to the back, giving them a warning as they scrambled to get in the bed. Feeling better, Charlie lay down and began to daydream about things she wanted to do on summer break.

"I love you, Charlie poop," Jodie said.

"I love you, too, beautiful toad," responded Charlie with a soft giggle and then they were both fast asleep.

It was finally Friday and the kids were happy that the weekend was approaching. Charlie wasn't as enthusiastic about her new teacher as she was the day before. She couldn't help but think he liked Jodie more than he did her. Jodie wasn't smarter than her or as funny as her. Jodie was only prettier than her and not by much. Charlie knew that teachers had their favorites, but good Lord; Jodie wasn't even in Mr. Frye's class. Maybe he just told Jodie about mom because she was older and assumed Jodie would better understand whatever he told her. On the other hand, Charlie knew it didn't matter because whatever he told Jodie about mom, Jodie would tell her.

Once school was over, Charlie went to meet up with Jodie and Joey outside by the school gymnasium. By the time she rounded the corner, she saw one of Joey's teachers standing with them with a big brown bag in her hand.

"Hey Charlie!" Jodie said as she ran up to her. "Guess what?"

"What?"

"Joey won the brown bag special in his class today!"

"What's the brown bag special?"

"It's fresh tomatoes, bell peppers, onions, carrots, and potatoes from Ms. Noel's garden."

Ms. Noel was the fourth-grade science teacher who had a green thumb. She would sporadically bring vegetables and fruits to school and one lucky kid in her class would win the collection in a drawing. Science was the only class Joey liked, so it was no surprise when he won.

Almost as if he had heard his name, Mr. Frye walked around the corner swinging his keys around his finger. Charlie began to wonder was he following them around the school. Why did he just seem to pop up when they were all together? Mr. Frye's humorous persona soon began to turn into annoyance.

"Hey kids. I found out in the teachers' lounge that little Joey won the brown bag surprise. Congratulations, sport!" He said, rubbing Joey's head.

"Yeah, I'm normally always in trouble, but not this time," Joey gleamed.

"Well, I'll be more than happy to give you guys a lift," offered Mr. Frye.

"No, we're taking the bus," blurted Charlie.

"Charlie, that's not polite. Sure, Mr. Frye, just drop us off where you left us the other day."

"Will do, I just have to stop by my house first."

"Jodie, you know grandma ain't about to play with us being late."

"It's fine, Charlie, trust me."

"No, I'm riding the bus," Charlie argued, storming off from them.

"Charlie, wait." Jodie said, catching up with her. "What's the real problem?"

Charlie couldn't admit that she was upset that her teacher seemed to favor her. It wasn't fair that everyone seemed to like Jodie. Joey had his science teacher, and they all had Grandma. Why couldn't Charlie have one person to herself?

"He's just becoming a weirdo and I don't like it."

"Yeah, but don't you wanna know about momma?"

"Yeah, but-"

"Come on, Charlie poop, I got this. We'll be home before grandma even knows anything."

Charlie was skeptical as she allowed Jodie to grab her hand as she followed her older sister. There was an eerie feeling running through Charlie's veins that she just couldn't shake. It didn't take being a psychic for Charlie to sense something was about to go wrong.

Chapter 4

"You two wait in the car while Jodie and I go fetch the pictures that I have of your mother." Mr. Frye said, looking back at Charlie and Joey.

"Why can't we go?" Joey asked.

"Because it will only take a few seconds. Besides, Jodie is older. She'll know what to look for."

"So, are you quickly grabbing something or looking for something?" Charlie questioned.

Mr. Frye squinted his eyes as if he was trying to intimidate Charlie. With a slight neck roll, Charlie folded her arms, waiting on the answer.

"Come on you guys. No more questions. We gotta make it home before grandma gets there." Jodie pleaded, opening her passenger door.

"Well, hurry back. There's no telling what may happen when you leave two kids alone," challenged Charlie.

Mr. Frye slammed his door as Charlie watched Jodie disappear in the house behind him. It was at that instance where Charlie knew she hated Mr. Frye. He was a liar who made up things as he went along. He also seemed to be a stalker. Suddenly, her grandmother's words echoed through her mind again. Beware of the men in trench coats. Charlie felt panicked, but she didn't want Joey to see her worried, so she stayed silent.

"Mr. Frye is a real slim-ball for leaving us out here alone," Joey began.

What felt like twenty minutes were probably only about five or six, but Joey was right. What if someone came by and decided to kidnap them? What if they weren't the well-behaved kids that grandma had taught them to be and they ran off somewhere?"

"It's okay, Joey. You have me to protect you."

"Well, who's gonna protect you since Jodie is in there?"

"You," she said and smiled, rubbing his head.

Another ten minutes had passed by and Charlie knew if they didn't leave soon that they wouldn't make it home before grandma. She looked over at Joey who was now playing with his prize bag. Whatever so-called pictures Mr. Frye was trying to find wasn't worth the switch that grandma would put on their hind-parts.

"You wait here, Joey, I'm going to go get Jodie."

"No!" He quickly protested, "You can't leave me here by myself."

"Okay, but you gotta keep quiet."

Charlie and Joey got out of the car and lightly closed the door. They tiptoed through the backyard and went in the same door that they saw Jodie enter. It was very quiet, almost like a creepy quiet as they crept past the kitchen into a hallway that led into more rooms and a staircase.

"They must be up those stairs," whispered Joey.

Charlie swallowed hard because she knew he was probably right. She wanted to call Jodie's name, but she was just as afraid as Joey who was now clinging on to her shirt. They slowly moved up the narrow stairway surrounded by walls on each side. Once they made it to the top, there were three separate doors that were all slightly closed.

Charlie put her finger up to her mouth and motioned for Joey to be quiet as she put her ear up to the first door. She didn't hear anything, so she slowly walked over to the next door with Joey still carefully moving behind her.

"Why aren't they talking?" Joey softly whispered.

Charlie shrugged her shoulders, not wanting to encourage Joey to continue to ask questions. The truth was she didn't know. *Why weren't they talking* wondered Charlie? Her heart began to race as a horrific thought had crossed her mind. What if Jodie's mouth was duct-taped and she was tied to a chair. Even worse, what if he had murdered Jodie and Mr. Frye was in the room chopping her up into little pieces.

Charlie's thoughts were quickly interrupted as she heard someone speak. She looked at Joey who pointed at the room where he thought he had heard the voice. Without thinking, Charlie walked forward and opened the door. She stood motionless as she saw Mr. Frye raise his face from Jodie's private area.

"Hey, you kids were supposed to stay in the damn car!" He yelled.

Charlie covered Joey's eyes, grabbed his hand, and ran out of the room. Once she made it outside, she had to stop and catch her breath. She bent over toward the ground, trying not to cry in order to protect Joey.

"Uh...Charlie? Are you okay?"

"Yes, Joey. I'm just a little scared, that's all."

"Did Jodie let Mr. Frye do that to her?"

"I don't know, Joey."

"Did she like it?"

"I don't know, Joey."

Mr. Frye barged out of his back door as if someone was after him and stopped in front of Joey and Charlie. Jodie slowly followed behind him with her head down. She didn't even look their way. She remained silent as she walked toward the car.

"Now, you listen here, you little shits," he said, pointing his finger in Charlie's face, "you better not tell anybody about what you saw, or I'll come after you."

"Hey, you get your dirty finger out of my sister's face," Joey challenged.

"Oh yeah...and what are you going to do if I don't," he said, walking up to Joey and mugging him to the ground.

Charlie was enraged. The only person she allowed to put their hands on Joey was grandma. She couldn't control her emotions.

"Don't ever put your hands on my brother again. If you do, I will find a way to kill you myself," she threatened.

Mr. Frye looked at her and let out a fake laugh. Charlie's demeanor was unchanged. Her voice had even changed when she said it. Joey looked up at Charlie as if she was a stranger. She stood there with her fist balled up as if she was ready to attack.

"You think I'm supposed to be afraid of a child," he said, purposely bumping into Charlie and walking toward the car. "Get your little asses in here."

Charlie gave Mr. Frye a death stare through his rear view mirror the entire ride home. It wasn't clear if he was annoyed or paranoid, but it made him uncomfortable. Even when he threatened to put her out of the car, she didn't cease her gaze. It was almost like she was in some type of evil trance. Whether she meant she'd try to kill him or if she was just being an irksome kid, her behavior was very peculiar for someone that age.

Mr. Frye stopped at the corner of their road like he did the last time. He placed his hand on Jodie's arm and asked was she okay. Without responding, Jodie quickly got out of the car and ran towards their house. This infuriated Charlie even more. She still hadn't moved.

"Come on Charlie, let's go," Joey pleaded, pulling her arm.

She finally climbed out of the car, turned around, and gave Mr. Frye an evil glare. He laughed as he began squalling his tires to get dust in her face. Charlie didn't realize how much she could hate a human being. She knew school was going to be awkward come Monday, and she wasn't sure how she was going to handle being in Mr. Frye's classroom. Although it was a huge issue, it was secondary to what just happened to her older sister. *Why would a grown man want to do that to a child* she wondered? *Did Mr. Frye make her do that or was Jodie just embarrassed that she got caught?* It was hard for Charlie to comprehend what had just happened. Even worse, what was grandma going to do to them if she found out about it?

Chapter 5

The kids weren't sure what to say to one another about the incident. They tried to act as normal as possible by getting cleaned up before grandma got home. Charlie watched Jodie as she sat on the bed, staring out the window. Charlie was certain that Jody didn't want grandma to know anything about what happened. Grandma would obviously know something was wrong if she continued to sit there like a frog on a log, so Jodie had to get herself together. Coincidentally, Grandma Rose hadn't made it home yet, so she must've had to work overtime.

"Uh Jodie, grandma will be home soon."

"So," she dryly responded.

"Well, it's going to be hard to hide something from grandma if you're hiding in this room."

"I'm not hiding, Charlie. I'll be in the kitchen when it's dinner time. You can tell her I'm doing homework until then."

"Are you okay? Did he hurt you?"

"I don't want to talk about it."

"Did he force you to let him go down there?"

"I said I don't want to talk about it," Jodie said a little firmer.

"If you don't talk about it, Jodie, you're going to be miserable for the rest of your life."

"Leave me alone, Charlie."

"Okay, but you can't say I didn't try."

Charlie walked out of the room and almost ran into Joey who was listening by the door. She was annoyed and hurt that Jodie didn't want to talk to her.

"What did she say?" He asked.

"She said nothing."

"Well, why wouldn't she talk to you?" Joey innocently asked, closely following Charlie.

"Leave me alone, Joey."

It was clear that Charlie had hurt his feelings, but so were hers. The vibe was unusual, and no one was talking. They were all spaced out in separate rooms. Sure enough, grandma walked through the door looking exhausted.

"Charlie, come grab this bag for me," Grandma Rose said.

Charlie put down her book and did as her grandma told her to. She walked into the kitchen and looked at Joey who was sulking. He had his elbows on the table with his head between his hands. It was obvious that he wanted someone's attention and he was surely about to get it.

"Why the long face, boy?" Grandma asked, following behind Charlie.

"Jodie is being mean to us."

"Jodie, come here," called grandma.

Charlie's heart began to flutter. A weird feeling began to emerge in her spirit. It was almost as if she knew their lives were about to change. She told them they had to act normal if they didn't want grandma to find out about it. But now it was too late.

"Yes, ma'am," Jodie responded, twisting her fingers, not knowing what had been said.

"What's going on with Joey?"

"I... I was upset that one of my friends called me a bad name at school and I took it out on Charlie and Joey. I'm sorry you guys."

Charlie was taken off guard, but very impressed by Jodie's ability to lie so quickly. It was almost as if she had practiced it. It made Charlie wonder what else she had lied so good about.

"I've told you a million times not to pay attention to those little heifers at school, now didn't I?"

"Yes ma'am, grandma," replied Jodie as her lips began to quiver.

Jodie almost got away with it until the tears began to form in her eyes. *How stupid can she be* thought Charlie? Grandma was smart enough to know that Jodie wouldn't be crying over something another girl had said. Hell, Jodie was one of the prettiest if not the prettiest girl at the school. Fortunate for Jodie, grandma didn't say anything. She just looked at all three children with suspicion and began preparing dinner.

An hour had passed, and they were all sitting at the dinner table. This was the first time ever that Charlie could recall the table being so silent during any meal. They normally got a special dessert on Fridays, but from the way grandma ate in silence, they probably weren't getting anything. Just as Charlie's thoughts flowed in, grandma's voice cut right through them.

"So... who's going to tell me what really happened?" Grandma asked, placing her fork in her plate.

No one made a sound. Charlie and Joey looked at each other and then at Jodie. She made no eye contact with her two siblings as her head hung low.

"Okay...Well, I guess no one gets dessert and everyone's getting skinned tonight with the switch."

There was a frown that came across Joey's face that Charlie hadn't seen in a while. He was glaring at Jodie as if he wanted to strike her. Charlie couldn't blame him. It became apparent that their older sister had no interest in protecting them, not even in her own mess.

"Jodie let Mr. Frye put his head between her legs," Joey blurted.

Jodie finally looked up and all eyes were on grandma. Joey quickly covered his mouth as if he accidentally let it slip. Grandma Rose closed her eyes as she took a deep breath and sighed. No one knew what to say as they saw a tear roll down grandma's face a few minutes later. It was hurt and shock at the same time because they had never seen her cry, not even when Uncle Benny died.

"Charlie, Joey, it's bedtime. Turn that light off and do not come out until I say so," Grandma Rose demanded with her eyes still closed. Grandma's tone was soft yet stern. They normally got to stay up late on Friday but not tonight. Without any questions Charlie did as she was told. They slowly walked past Jodie who was still transfixed on grandma. Charlie had the urge to reach out and hug her but was halted by fear.

"What do you think grandma is going to do to her," whispered Joey once their door was closed.

"I don't know, Joey."

"Do you think she'll hate me for telling on her?"

"Would you hate her if she told on you?"

"No, but I'd be mad as hell."

"Well, I guess she'll be mad as hell for a while."

"What do you think grandma is going to do to her?"

"Do you remember when we took the eggs from grandma's chicken coop and played baseball with them?" She asked.

"Yeah, that was pretty dumb," he replied and snickered.

"It wasn't funny when we were getting our butts whipped over and over, now was it?"

"No, but it's different when we get in trouble together. Grandma has to divide her energy."

"Perhaps you should have thought about that before telling on Jodie."

"It was your idea to go in there in the first place, Charlie."

"No, it was my idea to ride the bus, but you and Jodie insisted on going with that man."

"Well…well…you guys are older and should have known better."

"Whatever, Joey, goodnight."

Charlie turned away from Joey towards the wall. He had a point. Had she not made Joey follow her, they would have missed it all. She also should have been sterner about riding the bus. On the other hand, Charlie knew it was wrong for her teacher to do what he did to her sister. He deserved to be punished, not Jodie. She only hoped that Grandma Rose would see it that way.

Chapter 6

Charlie wasn't sure what time it was when she was awakened by a ruffling of the covers. She heard Jodie uncontrollably sniffing as she crawled into the bed. Charlie didn't say anything. She was just happy that Jodie lived through her punishment. A few minutes later, they both jumped as they heard the screen door to the front slam shut. They looked at each other and then Joey who was still fast asleep. Perhaps grandma was just going outside to think about her alternatives. She probably feared for Jodie's safety if Jodie returned to their school. It was the only school in the area for the next 25 miles. The police weren't expeditious when it came to handling reports in poor communities, especially black ones, so that was another dead end. On the other hand, perhaps grandma told Jodie what she was going to do. And if she did, Jodie was surely keeping her mouth shut.

The weekend had gone by and things had almost returned to normal. All the kids were talking again and no one brought up Jodie's incident. Grandma Rose seemed aloof at times; Charlie figured that she was still worried about Jodie going to school tomorrow. She probably told Jodie to avoid Mr. Frye at all cost and scream if he tried to approach her. Charlie also noticed that Grandma Rose had a bad burn on her hand, but it wouldn't be the first time she had picked up a pan that was too hot.

The next day, Charlie hadn't realized how nervous she would be once she got off the bus at school. How was she going to sit in a class with Mr. Frye knowing what he had done? The more she thought about it, the sicker she felt. She wished he would just disappear. Jodie must have noticed the apprehensive look on her face because she hugged her and then gave her a quick kiss on the forehead. Jodie promised her everything was going to be okay before disappearing down the hall.

Charlie walked in the opposite direction toward her classroom. She stopped at the door and slowly peeped around the corner to see if he was sitting at the desk. It was empty. She proceeded to walk to her desk with her head down to avoid any eye contact.

"What's wrong with you, Charlie?" A classmate asked after she sat down.

Before Charlie could answer the school's assistant principal, Mrs. Bowman walked into the room.

"Be quiet please and take your seats. Mr. Frye will not be joining us. There was an unfortunate accident over the weekend and Mrs. Joiner will be filling in until further notice."

"What happened to Mr. Frye?" A student asked.

"I heard he was burned alive in his home." Another student said, using a creepy voice.

"Settle down, children," Mrs. Bowman stated as the class began to talk at once.

"Well... Is he alive, Mrs. Bowman?" Charlie asked, unable to suppress her curiosity.

"He's in the hospital but no further details were given. You're more than welcome to say a silent prayer for him and class will resume as normal," Mrs. Bowman said, leaving the room.

Charlie was confused by the news. She wasn't sure if she felt good or bad about Mr. Frye being in a fire. She did just wish for him to disappear, but she didn't think it would happen that soon. Her sister seemed so positive that everything would work out, so she wondered if Jodie already knew about the news.

After what seemed like the longest day ever of school, Charlie got off the bus still perplexed about what had happened to Mr. Frye. She wanted to ask Jodie had she heard anything regarding the fire, but she didn't want to ask around Joey. Once they walked through the door, they were all startled to see Grandma Rose lying on the couch. She let out a harrowing cough as she spat in a can.

"Grandma, are you okay?" Joey asked, crouching down as he gently grabbed her hand.

A warm smile had crossed grandma's face. She grabbed Joey by the ear and pulled him close while whispering something to him.

After she was done, Joey nodded his head and went back to the back.

"Jodie, I need a minute alone with Charlie. I want you to go and sit with your brother."

Jodie kissed Grandma Rose on the forehead and went back to the back with Joey. An overwhelming feeling of dread had overcome Charlie. She had never seen grandma so vulnerable and powerless. All these sudden changes in events had baffled Charlie. Her world had turned upside down in the course of a few days.

"Grandma is getting old, Charlie, and I'm going to need you to step up to the plate."

"I don't understand, Grandma. You were fine just the other day. What's wrong?"

"Sometimes people do things in order to protect others. As a parent, you always want your kids to have a better life than what you had. Your mother did what she thought was best and so have I under the circumstances. But one thing I want you to always remember, Charlie, is no matter who or what you are protecting, you must reap what you sow."

Charlie knew what grandma said required no further explanation. It had to have been her. Grandma must have left that night after talking to Jodie and burned down Mr. Frye's home. It would explain the burn on her hand and the wicked coughs.

"What's going to happen to us, grandma?" Charlie asked with tears in her eyes.

"Sweetheart, you're going to be fine. I expect for you to do great things, Charlie. I want you to be a leader."

"But grandma, I have a boy's name. People will take me for a joke."

"Don't be silly, Charlie, that's not true. I remem
mother was pregnant with you and she complained al.
constantly moving around and not allowing her to slee
you were a busy body, but I told her you were trying to
everything you could from the outside world. She wanted to name
you Joylynn after your sister, but I said no. Even then I could sense
the greatness in you, so I named you after your great grandfather
Charles Johnson, who was the first black defense attorney in our
hometown."

"Wow, I never knew that, grandma."

"I want you to help take care of your younger brother and older
sister. Your ability to retain and utilize information is a lot different
from theirs."

"Okay grandma, I will. What's going to happen to you?"

"My soul will soon be at rest, baby. My love for you children
will always be here in spirit. If you find yourself feeling confused or
lonely, just go to a quiet room and talk to Jesus. He will send me to
comfort you."

"Will momma be able to comfort us, too?"

Charlie knew this would be the only time she could ask about
their mother. Charlie had assumed her mother had died a long time
ago until Mr. Frye claimed that he had information about her. It was
time to get closure.

"Charlie, your mother loved you, your brother, and your sister
very much. I know deep down in my heart that if there was a way for
her to get back to you guys, she would."

"So, she's not dead?"

We don't know, Sweetie. No one has seen or heard from her in a few years. A missing person report was filed, but then the case went cold."

"Shouldn't we give up hope by now, grandma? A few years is a long time."

Grandma Rose was at a loss for words as tears welled up in her eyes. It wasn't hard for Charlie to decipher what she was saying. Their mother would never leave them for years unless she was in jail or dead. Law enforcement would know if they had her in their custody, so that left only one other option. Grandma just couldn't allow herself to admit it.

"It's okay, grandma. We know that you love us, and I want you to know that we love you so much." Charlie said as she gave her a hug.

Unfortunately, Grandma Rose had gotten weaker as the days passed. Jodie had missed about a week of school to help grandma around the house. One day after returning home from school, Charlie and Joey found Jodie sitting in front of Grandma Rose crying. She lay there peacefully on her bed and her skin was cold to the touch. Charlie walked out of the room and called Aunt Jane as her grandma had instructed her a few days ago. Charlie went outside and sat alone on the edge of the porch. She folded her arms together and looked up at the sky.

"I need you two right now," she said as she closed her eyes and let the tear fall down her cheeks.

(Time Lapse)

Chapter 7

"Hey sis, what's going on?" Joey asked, walking into Charlie's office.

"I'm not taking another one of your associate's cases, Joey."

"Wow, really sis?" He questioned and laughed. "Is it like that?"

"Joey, I have a lot of work to do and I can no longer continue to accept cash from clients with unaccountable resources."

"Charlie, let's be realistic. We both know that my clients helped pay more than half of your tuition to even get you here."

"Leave it to you to never play it down."

"Sis, I didn't come by to gloat or ask you for any favors. I just came by to check on you and see had you heard from Reece, that's all."

"Yeah, I'm sure I would be the first person she calls since I helped you get custody of Royce."

"Is the sarcasm necessary, Charlie? Besides, it's not like we didn't do the right thing. She left my son alone in the house for damn near two days."

"To me, it sounded like her defense that it was a misunderstanding between her and the housekeeper was probable. Besides, you knew what she did before you met her."

"So, you're taking an addict's side over me and your four-year-old nephew?"

"He wasn't harmed, and he loves his mom. Yes, she was irresponsible and she needs help, but I can't say I believe it was intentional."

"It doesn't matter. What if he would have fallen down the stairs or electrocuted himself?"

"Those are accidents that could happen even when adults are there."

"I feel like you're questioning my parenting all of a sudden. What's up with that?"

"Of course not, Joey. Where is my love bug now?"

"He's...he's safe."

"Okay then. He's safe in your custody and all is well. Reece should be your last concern."

"Look, I was just seeing did she contact you. Royce has been asking about her. He misses his mom."

"With all the maids and housekeepers you have, how could he?"

"Listen, if she happens to contact you please let her know her son asked about her, I'm out." He said, walking towards the door. "Oh, you need to contact your sister. She's changed her name again and gone international," he added, firmly shutting the door.

Lately, Charlie felt overwhelmed after having any conversation with Joey. She hated when he constantly reminded her of how he paid the law school tuition that financial aid didn't cover. Him making her feel like she owed him her career put a wedge in their relationship.

Charlie always thought her and Joey's bond would be unbreakable. Even after their grandmother's death, they stuck to each other like glue. They protected one another from their aunt's children. Although their aunt claimed that she was doing the best she could, considering she was already raising two kids of her own, her kids were a constant nuisance.

Their cousins started fights for no reason and would do mean things like cut holes in Joey's and Charlie's clothing. Their older cousin Nathan seemed to have had a crush on Jodie because he was always picking on her. Aunt Jane worked two full-time jobs, so she was practically never home. Charlie and Joey made sure that Jodie was never in a position where she was alone with Nathan, which started most of the fights.

After two years of instability, Jodie ran away when she turned sixteen. Strangely enough, the fighting stopped, but Joey became distant. He started hanging with the street crowd and selling drugs. He was in and out the juvenile court system and jail over the course of about fifteen years.

Now that they were adults, Joey was arrogant and acted like a pompous jerk at times. He was no longer the caring little brother she once knew. Even though Charlie knew he loved her, he didn't consider how his actions and words affected others.

He somehow obtained ownership of a farm out in the rural area that allowed him to cover his massive drug trafficking operation. Although he had told Charlie he was legit since he opened his farming business, Charlie still didn't believe he was completely done with his underground lifestyle. He managed to stay out of jail for the last four years and him not flaunting his wealth definitely helped. Joey's main problem was women. Well, one woman in particular, Reece Summers.

Charlie knew that she didn't have time to concern herself with Joey's personal affairs. She had to call Jodie to see what the hell Joey meant by her going international.

"Excuse me, Ms. Johnson, your next appointment has arrived," the office secretary said, peeking her head in the door.

Charlie had totally forgotten that she had scheduled the late meeting with a new client last Friday. She canceled her call to her sister and pulled out her new client's file. His name was Winston Hughes. Charlie giggled because she remembered how she thought his name sounded like an ancient famous writer when she first had heard it.

A moment later, a tall dark man in a suit walked through her door. He had a short haircut and his goatee was perfectly aligned. He looked nothing short of a model in an Ebony magazine. Charlie found him very attractive, but she had to keep a professional face.

"Hello, I am Charlie Johnson," she said as she cleared her throat.

He walked over to meet her gesture for a handshake as she offered him to have a seat.

"Hello Ms. Johnson, I am very pleased to meet you. I also wanted to thank you for getting me in on such a short notice."

"It's no problem. It's all a part of the job. My secretary briefed me on your case, but I would like to get the full details from you, Mr. Hughes."

"Well... I thought I was happily married to a beautiful woman. She was the love of my life and I planned on having kids with her."

"Okay, this definitely starts off as the all-American dream." Charlie said.

"I know, right? But unfortunately for me, it became a nightmare. Three months after the marriage, she took all the funds out of our joint account, sold the new Porsche that were in both our names, and took off with my inheritance of my great grandmother's jewelry worth a half million dollars. My ancestors died in those mines they were forced to work in for those jewels."

"Did you sign a prenup?"

He shifted in his chair as he grew silent. The look in his eyes had already answered the question. He placed his elbow on the armrest and covered his fist over his mouth.

"This is why I need your help. I heard you were the best and the best is what I need."

"I don't give my clients false hope. Even if you take her to court, more than likely she's going to say that everything was a gift."

"Why would I give her something that has been passed down by my family from generation to generation?"

"And her defense will say because she is your wife and you wanted to lavish her with jewels and diamonds."

"I bought her things separately. I never allowed her to even wear those jewels. I had all this way before the marriage."

"We just may have something. Community property is the property that is obtained during the marriage by either party. This probably would fall under your joint bank account and the car. However, your inheritance will likely be considered as separate property as long as the property was assigned solely to you."

"I just want my family legacy back and my half of what I put into that account."

"What was her response when you reached out to her?"

"I couldn't get in contact with her. She changed her number and quit her job!"

"Did you try to contact her family or close friends?"

"She told me her parents were dead and she was an only child. We actually rented bridesmaids for our wedding."

"How long did you know this woman?"

"We dated six months, we were engaged an additional two, and then we got married."

"Did something happen after you two were married that would cause her to flee?"

"Look, Ms. Johnson, I'm looking for a lawyer, not a counselor."

"And as your potential lawyer I suggest you tell me everything I'm up against because I refuse to look like some half-witted nincompoop in front of the judge," she fired back.

"I'm sorry. I'm just angry. I didn't think Bria Ray would do this."

Charlie cringed. She knew exactly who Bria Ray was.

Chapter 8

After using a clever excuse to rush Winston out of her office,
Charlie waited until she got into her Lexus before calling Jodie. She
needed time to think about what just happened. How did this man
know she had any connection whatsoever to that name? It was hard
for her to believe that him walking into her office was by sheer
coincidence. Her initial thought was it was a set up or some type of
joke someone was playing on her. But the look on Winston's face
said he was serious. She wasn't quite sure how Jodie was involved,
but she knew that Jodie knew something. Charlie couldn't remember
the details, but she recalled overhearing Jodie say the name Bria Ray
in more than a few past phone conversations.

Charlie knew she had a name for herself as one of the best lawyers in town, but she still couldn't understand how Winston could link her to Jodie. Charlie had the law firm website, but Jodie wasn't even on social media. They rarely had the chance to hang out with each other and Jodie rarely used her real name. Hell, they didn't even reside in the same state. Besides, this mystery woman Winston told her about said she didn't have any siblings. Although this information softened the blow a little, Jodie could really be in deep shit, even if it was by association. Just as she was about to call Jodie, her cell phone rang.

"Hi, Charlie, it's Reece."

"Hello Reece. How are you?"

"I'm just peachy. I'm as peachy as a mother without her child could be."

"I can imagine." Charlie sarcastically responded. "Well, you kind of caught me at a bad time. I have some serious things that I need to attend to."

"Yes, your time is always precious, Charlie. Lord forbid if anyone interrupts you from your precious business. Speaking of precious, do you know how much I miss my precious baby boy?"

"Oh my gosh, Reece. Why do you keep calling me over this nonsense? You and my brother are two adults who should be able to learn how to properly co-parent. Besides, you have visitation rights. Just go and see him, for crying out loud."

"That poor excuse for a brother of yours won't allow me to take my son anywhere. Do you know how it feels to see your child for two hours twice a week? Oh, you wouldn't know because you can't even keep a man to even have a child."

"Reece, the last thing you should ever worry about is my personal life. I suggest that we keep this conversation professional since I have no intention of shaming you on this phone. Now, the two-hour a week visitation was the judge's order, not his."

"I know you two losers petitioned for it. I'm sure he's probably fucking the judge too and you may even be dyking with her."

"Listen, truth be told, you left your son at home alone to get a fix and to follow that quote, poor excuse for a brother of mine. You must be high as hell now to think you can call your baby's daddy attorney and harass me. If you love your son that much, then rehab should be a no-brainer. Get your life together and stop blaming everyone else for being an unfit mother."

"A motherless child and a childless woman could never understand. Let this be the last time you and that thot sister of yours try to judge me. Oh and uh...by the way, I hope you know I'm taking him back to court since he missed two visitations where the ruling clearly states he has to be present, not his house whores. See you in court."

As Charlie hung up, she could feel the blood boiling in her veins as her blood pressure soared. She would never let Reece know, but Joey's priorities were definitely mismanaged. She was sick and tired of covering up for her siblings. Every time she turned around she was getting their asses out of something. It was almost like they were still kids in the mind. Charlie wasn't sure how much more she could handle. On top of it all, she still had to check in with Jodie.

"Hey Charlie poop, what's good?"

"What's good? You can't be seriously asking me this right now, Jodie?"

"Charlie, you should really go out more and work less. You're constantly nagging with no one to nag."

"My personal affairs are in check. It's too bad I can't say the same thing about you and your damn brother."

"Oh gosh. What's wrong now, Charlie?" Jodie asked condescendingly.

"Well, I don't know, Jodie. I was seeing why some stranger was in my office wanting me to take a case against Bria Ray."

"Charlie!"

"Don't Charlie me. I'm sick and tired of you and Joey's bullshit."

"Well, aren't we the reason grandma wanted you to become a lawyer? Didn't she want you to protect us?"

"Not when you're purposely fucking up!" Charlie yelled.

"Calm down, Charlie poop. You're going to have another anxiety attack."

"Jodie, this is not a game. I need to know everything there is to know about Bria Ray."

"Charlie, there is nothing to know and you cannot take the case."

"I suggest you get to talking instead of telling me what I can or can't do."

"Charlie, I'm not in a position where I can discuss your case with you right now." Jodie said, now changing the tone of her voice as Charlie heard a male voice in the background. "Hey, big daddy.

I'm just talking with my sister. I'll be back down in a minute. Go get the hot tub ready for us."

"Are you serious right now?" Charlie asked, completely annoyed.

"Look, I'm spending quality time with the love of my life, so I have to have sister time with you later and we can talk about anything that you want." Jodie explained.

"Meet me at my house tomorrow at noon."

"Charlie, I'm not six hours away. I am halfway across the freaking world with Santana."

"I don't give a damn if you're with Julio Iglesias. Have your ass at my house by this weekend," Charlie demanded and hung up her phone.

Once Charlie made it home, she went straight into the kitchen and poured her a glass of wine. Jodie had done some pretty dumb things in her lifetime but this had to be the dumbest. She wasn't sure if Jodie changed her name to swindle this guy or if it was one of her idiot girlfriends who Charlie called moronic tricks.

Jodie and her so-called "Malicious Madams" all worked together duping men out of money. They normally dealt with married men for obvious reasons, but greed began to consume them. One of Jodie's friends had a dad that is a police chief, so the girls started exploiting drug dealers by saying they could help protect them. Charlie had warned her sister that karma was a bitch and she needed to change her lifestyle. She even begged Jodie to come work in her office, but every time Jodie was a no show.

Jodie was addicted to the fast money, flashy cars, and material things. But this time, someone chose the wrong man. Winston Hughes was just as mysterious as he was handsome. He was too clean-cut and articulate to be just some guy that would lie down and take a loss. He made certain that Charlie knew that his family died for those possessions. In Charlie's mind, it meant he just may kill for them as well.

Chapter 9

A few days later Jodie arrived at Charlie's house around two in the afternoon in her drop-top Mercedes Benz. She wore a navy blue, flowered sundress with a tan sun hat and shades. She carried a Shih Tzu in a large Louis Vuitton bag that was strapped around her shoulder. It was one of the most appalling shit-show renditions of the Hollywood lifestyle that Charlie had ever seen.

"Hello, Charlie. You look business-like as usual." Jodie said, walking through the door.

"Put that little thing out back," Charlie demanded, "and he better not shit on my flowers."

"Wow Charlie, it looks like an oasis out here! So, this is where you spend all your time and hard-earned money, I see."

"Just try not to get your handprints all over my glass doors."

"What else do you have to do besides clean and work?"

"Let's not take cheap shots, Miss Marilyn Mon-no."

"Charlie, please. Marilyn Monroe didn't have shit on me. Besides, I'm only looking out for your best interest. You need that strong, muscular man holding you in his arms and pushing that long, thick penis between your legs. Your anxiety attacks will cease and your stress levels would be cut in half. You do know that stress can kill you, right?"

"Getting dicked-down isn't going to prevent the stupid shit you and your brother put me through."

"We live the way we want to live, so why can't you just let us be."

"I can't just let you guys be when Reece is constantly harassing me over Royce, and a strange man comes into my office about being ripped off by one of you Barbies!"

"Reece is just a cunt that wants redemption for her tragic life by trying to steal my nephew."

"Well, that is his mother and you weren't saying that about her when she was working with you."

"Whose side are you on, Charlie?"

"Oh my gosh, if I didn't know any better I would swear you and your brother were twins."

"Well, you do always take up for her."

"No, I just tell you two the truth. Yes, she has some serious problems, but you two were once all up in her ass until she stopped doing what y'all wanted her to do."

"Whatever. I'm not going to spend my weekend discussing some useless speck of a mother. Who is this man asking about Bria Ray?"

"First of all, is Bria Ray one of your many aliases?"

"No, Charlie."

"Really?" Charlie suspiciously asked, folding her arms.

"Have I ever lied to you?"

"Do you remember that time I asked you did you know if grandma set that fire-"

"Charlie, we were still kids! Are you kidding me?" Jodie interrupted.

"A lie is a lie."

"Charlie, I can't with you today."

"Fine, then don't with me today. I'll just take his case since it's not you."

"Okay already...listen. Bria Ray is not a person. They are identical twins. One twin took the first three or so months and the other twin finished off the job."

"The job? What's the job?" Charlie questioned.

"What do you think? We take this guy for whatever we could."

"And you all feel good about yourself?"

"He is an arrogant prick who gets off from thinking he can buy women and treat them like trash. No, we don't feel guilty about going after these low-life, cheating husbands and these womanizers."

"It doesn't make it right, but my pity meter has gone down a little. I don't understand how he could not tell he was dealing with a different woman at some point?"

"Duh, they are identical twins, so it's not hard for one to imitate the other."

"Yeah, but everyone's spirit and reactions are different."

"Are you kidding me, Charlie? Guys don't care about shit like that. Besides, this man was so infatuated with their looks and sex that he probably wouldn't have cared even if he knew they had switched."

"So where do you fit into all of this, Jodie?"

"I took fifteen percent since I provided them with the guy and let them do whatever they wanted with the car."

"Jodie, this man seems dangerous. He is upset about the money in his bank account, but he is livid about the inheritance they took from him."

"It was a joint account. We're not stupid. We do find ways to cover our tracks, and his inheritance? What inheritance?"

"Wow, that's classic, Jodie. Stop acting like you don't know."

"I'm not acting like anything. I don't know anything about an inheritance."

"They stole this man's jewel inheritance worth over five hundred thousand dollars!"

"You'd better have the story mixed up for those bitches' sake," Jodie said, grabbing her phone.

Jodie went outside to make her phone call. Charlie was relieved that it wasn't Jodie who was physically with Winston, but she still played a part in the devious plan. She had told Jodie a million times that everyone and everything around her were ticking bombs of deceit waiting to explode. She thought Jodie would have learned her lesson when her ex-partner Reece had started dating their brother.

"I can't believe those ungrateful bitches hid half a million dollars from me. I want you to take the case and bury those lying skanks!" Jodie yelled, coming back into the living room.

"That sounds like a great idea. Did you think about the part where they accuse you of initiating everything and then paying you a fee? That's called extortion, Sweetheart."

"I don't care. I'm sick and tired of people thinking it's okay to run me over. I guess everyone thinks it's cool to take advantage of the pretty little light-skinned girl with no formal education. I'm not having it! They will pay."

"Do you really hear yourself, Jodie? Regardless if this man is a loser or not, y'all had no right to steal his shit. And for you to get upset because you were schemed by schemers is absurd."

"Can you stop being a lawyer and be my sister for one damn minute!"

"You want me to be a sister. Okay, I will be a sister. You sound ridiculous as hell trying to go after two ladies that you are for one, the ringleader of their dark enterprise. Two, the shit isn't yours to begin with, and three, your ass could end up in jail or worse. Then, there's the fact that what y'all do is immoral and will catch up with you!"

"Do you really want to talk about morals, Charlie? Where were morals when that grown man made me pull down my pants when I was a kid? Where were morals when grandma burned down the man's house and left us? Where were fucking morals when Aunt

Jane's boyfriend took my virginity? Where were mom's morals when she ran off with that man who ended up killing her? That's right, Charlie. I may have been a kid, but I was old enough to remember a little bit. She chose him and he ended up killing her in the long run. How do you like that shit for morals, Charlie? Huh? Me? I don't give a fuck about morals, Charlie." Jodie said, putting back on her shades and walking out of the front door.

It wasn't until minutes later that Charlie realized that Jodie had left her dog from its pawing at her back door. She was still traumatized by Jodie's confessions about Aunt Jane's boyfriend and the comments about their mother. All that time, Grandma Rose was protecting Charlie from the truth. Their mother had chosen to leave them. To add insult to injury, Charlie assumed that she and Joey were protecting Jodie from Nathan when they should have been protecting her from Nathan's stepdad. Charlie felt broken all over again. She didn't know what to think or what to do. What would grandma do? She sat there twitching her fingers. Perhaps it was time to get some answers about her mom and what happened to Jodie by paying Aunt Jane and her now husband a special visit.

Chapter 10

Later that evening, Charlie pondered about everything that Jodie had said. It was always the same thing with her. She never really expressed her feelings to anyone. Jodie had been keeping secret hurt inside since she was a kid. How did she expect anyone to help her if she never told anyone about her issues? Then it dawned on Charlie that they all held unresolved issues inside. What really happened to their mother? Why did grandma have to die for what she thought was protection for them? How did she end up getting a deadly amount of smoke in her lungs? Grandma Rose lying there lifeless had begun to replay in her mind as the tears rolled down her face.

Charlie's solemn moment was short-lived by a call from an unknown number. She let it go to voicemail to see if the caller would leave a message. Charlie was floored once she discovered the voicemail was left by none other than Winston Hughes. Charlie was beyond livid since no clients were allowed to have access to personal information. It was then when she realized that Winston had more connections than she had originally suspected. She called in a favor to one of her friends who worked for a private investigation firm. She had to know how Winston was getting her information.

The next day Charlie decided to call Jodie to check on her. She wanted to make sure she made it home safe, but she also wanted to see if she could find out more about this Winston character. Surprisingly, Jodie answered on the first ring.

"Oh, Charlie, I'm so glad you called," Jodie said in a whimpering tone.

"Jodie, it wasn't my intentions to upset you. Everything is going to be okay. I'll take care of your little doggie until you come back. I even bought a little kettle, doggie toys, and food for him...you know, the doggie works I guess."

"I knew he would be in great hands. His name is Mechè."

"I think I can remember that until you get here. Hey, I was also thinking that maybe you, me, and Joey could sit down as a family and talk to a counselor or-,"

"No, Charlie. I'm not upset. These are tears of joy. I'm happy and I want you to keep the dog."

"Oh, okay...Well, that's great, Sweetie."

"Yes, Charlie. I just got some great news!"

"What? You switched to Geico and saved money on your car insurance?"

"Oh, Charlie," she said as she laughed, "I've missed this silly side of you. It actually comes just in time."

"I'm sorry. I didn't know I was an insufferable bore all these years. What am I in time for?

"The sparkling side of your personality is just in time for your new niece or nephew."

"What?"

"Yes, Charlie. I'm pregnant!"

"Wow...wow!" Charlie repeated.

"Isn't this awesome? I was shocked at first, too. I kept thinking could I really be a good mother? Does someone like me have what it takes to raise an entire human being? I continued to doubt myself, but Santana was so loving and supportive. He gave me so much hope. His happiness about the baby made me happy. I'm done with the underground hustle life. Santana and this baby aren't worth the risk. Besides, I saw Santana looking at rings in his phone earlier today," Jodie softly shrieked.

"I have to admit, I'm a little shocked as well, but if you're happy I'm happy."

"Thank you, Charlie, for being there for me and for everything you've done."

After hanging up with Jodie, Charlie felt perplexed. Her relationship with her brother was already strained and now she felt like she was losing her sister. Jodie was starting a new family and all she had now was a dog. It was a dog that she felt was given to her out of pity to help with her loneliness. Charlie hadn't felt this inadequate in years.

After feeding Mechè, Charlie sat down at the table to have a snack. As her phone suddenly rang and vibrated on the table, Mechè let out a cute little bark. Charlie had actually found it amusing. She turned her attention back towards her phone and noticed she had received the call she had been waiting for from yesterday.

"Hey sis, I got the four-one-one on this Winston character," her friend said once Charlie answered.

"Girl, I don't know if I'm ready, but go ahead and indulge me."

"Everything that you may have suspected of this guy would probably be accurate. He is linked to a Mississippi drug lord, but my sources say he is a relative and not active in any drug-related activity. He was the sole heir to a mining company that was sold for two point three million dollars. He has a bad reputation for verbally and physically abusing women, which is why he was arrested a few years ago on an assault charge."

"Does he stay here in Georgia?"

"Not that I'm aware of. He has a home in Tallahassee, Florida and two condos in Waco, Texas."

"Do you have any idea as to how and why he would contact me?"

"Well, I didn't at first but when I checked his cell phone records, this one local phone number continued to show."

"Did you find out who it was?"

"I think you'll know when I give you the number. It's 555-0304."

It wasn't unbelievable, but it was definitely a head-spinner. Charlie couldn't believe this selfish bitch would put her family in danger yet again. Charlie thanked her friend and immediately set a plan into action. It was time to let Reece Summers know she was not the one to be played with.

It was a little after eight when Charlie sat down on the couch to watch a movie on Netflix. While flickering through the channels she received yet another unexpected phone call. However this time, Charlie knew exactly who it was calling.

"Hello, Aunt Jane? Is this you?"

"Hello, Charlie," she responded in a tiresome voice.

Charlie looked at her phone not knowing what to think. She hadn't spoken to her aunt since her aunt had kicked Joey out of her house about 15 years ago. Charlie had to move out of her college dorm in order to get an apartment with Joey.

"I wanted you to come and pick up a few things that were your mother's possessions."

"I don't understand. Why are you giving them to me now?"

"I feel that they belong to you."

"Oh, okay. I'll try to come down the weekend after next."

"No, Charlie. I need you to come tonight."

"What? Are you insane? I'm not coming down there tonight."

"I am dying...Charlie. I will not make it through the night."

Charlie looked at her phone again, not knowing if she believed what she had heard. Aunt Jane did sound awful, but maybe that was from all those years of working and not paying attention to her husband while he sexually assaulted her sister. Perhaps this would be her last chance to tell her the truth about that evil man. She agreed to the visit as she quickly ended the call.

Charlie looked at Mechè who was comfortably lying beside her on the couch. She put him in his kettle and gave him extra food as he whimpered while she went to grab her things. The call was so short and direct that it left Charlie suspicious. It was obvious why her aunt couldn't call Jodie or Joey, but why did she call her at such a strange hour. *Was she really dying*, Charlie wondered *or was this a host for selfish intentions*?

Chapter 11

Charlie lived about six hours away from her Aunt Jane's home, so she chartered a mini flight through one of her many connections. She was hesitant about making this trip on such a short notice, but Jodie had already stirred her spirit and Aunt Jane calling put the icing on the cake. She had to know if her aunt knew more than what she let on about her mother's death and to see exactly what things Aunt Jane claimed to have of her mother's items. She also wondered did Aunt Jane already know about her husband's wicked ways. Perhaps she was a part of the disgusting scheme and used her two jobs as a cover up for not knowing. Charlie grew even more suspicious of Aunt Jane as she thought about the possibilities. Furthermore, what was she going to do when she discovered the truth?

Charlie remembered that Grandma Rose had once mentioned that Aunt Jane and her mother didn't have the best relationship after they became adults, so it seemed weird that she would still have some of her mother's belongings. Aunt Jane wasn't even willing to cooperate with the police during the investigation of her missing sister. But somehow or the other grandma did make Aunt Jane promise to take care of them if something were to happen to her. Apparently, grandma's version of "take care" was obviously used loosely.

Charlie arrived in her rented car and slowly walked up to the porch of the old house. From the looks of the outside, nothing had changed. Although it was dark, there didn't seem to be any remodeling done and the shutters were literally falling off of the house. It was nothing short of a wreck in appearance as was Aunt Jane when she opened the door. Charlie was mortified.

"I saw your lights from the window." Aunt Jane said, opening the door. "I'm glad you made it down here. As you can see I look like hell. The doctors say it could be any day now, so I obviously wasn't lying if you thought I was."

"What was your diagnosis?" Charlie asked with a touch of sensitivity.

"Ah...various things from head to toe I guess. I've had two heart surgeries in the last five years and I've been on dialysis for a few years. Of course, you guys wouldn't know since you cut us off without warning."

"I guess it was similar to you allowing Jodie to run away and you kicking out Joey with no warning."

"Hmm...I guess I partially deserved that. I could've done more. But don't judge me if you've never unexpectedly had to raise five kids on one income."

"You actually had two jobs. One for you and for that looser who sat around the house and did nothing while you worked your ass off."

"It was hard back then, Charlie. No one wanted to give a job to a disabled man."

"That's bullshit and you know it. That man was fully capable of doing something besides allowing you to come home exhausted with aches and pains. The bastard wouldn't even cook for us. So, as strong and as dominate as you pretended to be, why didn't you wear the pants you were already wearing and make your sorry ass husband do something?" Charlie challenged.

"You watch your mouth, Charlie. Don't get ahead of yourself. I still took all three of you in when I could have just let you all go to social services and be split up in separate foster homes. You still owe me respect," she demanded as she pointed her finger.

"I apologize for disrespecting you, but I will not apologize for calling that poor excuse for a human a sorry ass loser."

To Charlie's surprise, Aunt Jane looked down and smirked. She took a deep breath and gathered her thoughts. She looked Charlie directly in the eyes as she spoke.

"You were always Rose's favorite, Charlie. She saw the passion and fire inside of you. She knew you would protect your brother and sister by any means and I'm willing to bet you're still sacrificing your happiness to do it now."

"Aunt Jane, I came down to briefly chat and get whatever you wanted to give me that belonged to my mom. You are in no position to analyze my life."

"You're right, I'm not. I think there comes a point in life where we all have to stop making excuses for ourselves. We may not want to agree with our past, but we definitely must come to terms with it. I've made a lot of mistakes, Charlie. But I do care for you kids."

"That's...that's good to know. We are grateful that you initially opened your home to us," Charlie responded, holding herself back from getting emotional.

"I want you to see something before you go."

Aunt Jane grabbed a lantern and told Charlie to follow her to the basement. Charlie was hesitant, but she slowly walked behind her. After passing a few rooms and a dingy kitchen, they made it to the basement door. Each step made a creaking noise as they approached the bottom of the stairs. Oddly enough, the basement appeared to be the nicest room in the house.

"What the hell is this?" Charlie yelled, horrified by what she saw.

"It's Jerry, Charlie. He's tied up to the bed."

Charlie cautiously surveyed Aunt Jane's husband lying on a bunk in the corner of the basement. He looked bruised and beaten while lying in a fetal position with patches covering his eyes. He had a tube coming from his stomach in addition to being on an oxygen machine. Charlie couldn't tell if he was dead or alive.

"He's been in bad shape for a while. He was diagnosed with stage four cancer a few months back. I prayed for him. I couldn't understand why God allowed him to suffer so much. That is...until Jodie called me last week. She told me she was moving on with her life, so she had to forgive Jerry for what he had done. You can imagine that I was embarrassed and humiliated when I heard the story. After not being able to get him to admit to what he had done, I slowly began to lessen his oxygen. As he gasped for air to fill his lungs, he confessed it all, Charlie. So, I beat him. I beat him until I was as tired as all those extra shifts I had worked. He used what little strength he had to try and wrestle with me. That's when-," she paused as her voice began to crack.

"That's when what?" Charlie asked.

"He had pushed me into the closet and I fell through an opening that was covered up by wallpaper. I would have never found it had I not fell through that wall."

"What did you find?"

"I found a box with women things in it and I remembered...I remembered," she said, now crying.

"I don't understand," Charlie responded.

"Not...not only did he have sex with my niece-," Aunt Jane stalled, exploding with emotion.

She fell down to the floor. Charlie didn't know what to say. She had never seen her so vulnerable and helpless. What else could this man have done that could be worse than this?

"Charlie!" She howled. "I found your mother's necklace and pearl earrings in a box he had been hiding all these damn years! These were the same things she had on when she went missing."

"Wh...what?" Charlie stammered, not sure if she heard her correctly.

"I asked him over and over how did he get her belongings and what did he do to her. The only answer he had was that she gave them to him and left. Joanna would never do that. She loved those pearls. Her daddy gave them to her before he died at war."

Charlie kneeled down beside her aunt and held her as she wailed. Although Charlie was devastated by the horrific confession, her aunt had to have been traumatized. The man she slept next to every night had raped her niece and likely killed her sister. He was truly the son of Lucifer. He deserved to die a painful death.

"I showered four times and I scrubbed myself until my skin turned red," Aunt Jane continued. "I knew that wasn't going to be enough. I knew there was only one way to have him gone for good."

Aunt Jane walked over to a dresser in the corner of the room. She lifted up a towel and pulled out a small pistol. Charlie gasped at the sight of the gun.

"What are you doing, Jane?"

"I wanted to make it right. I wanted him to pay for torturing my family and all those years that my momma suffered from not knowing what happened to her daughter. How could this man sleep beside me with no conscience? It's repulsive."

"I don't know, Aunt Jane." Charlie responded, standing stiff.

"I wanted to give you this opportunity. He took so much away from you kids. You have my permission, Charlie. Kill him."

Chapter 12

Charlie looked at her aunt as she held out the gun in front of her. She couldn't figure out her aunt's true intentions. Was she trying to play on her emotions by getting her to do her dirty work for her or was she sincere about offering her a chance at revenge? If he got shot, it would likely be investigated.

She surely would snitch out Charlie if it came down to one or the other going to prison. On the other hand, he did do some horrible things to the family. Maybe Aunt Jane had already dug his grave out back. It wasn't like anyone would miss him. From what Charlie had heard, his own kids had even disowned him. Perhaps Jerry may have even indirectly led Grandma Rose to burn down Mr. Frye's home.

Maybe Grandma Rose thought Mr. Frye would do something to the kids if he found out they had admitted what he did to Jodie. Grandma obviously wasn't going to risk losing another child, especially a grandchild. So many thoughts were running through Charlie's mind that she actually considered ending his life. Besides, she was a lawyer. She knew how to cover shit up to her advantage.

"What's it gonna be, Charlie?"

Charlie looked over at Jerry who appeared to still be knocked-out cold. Although she had no sympathy, he had clearly taken a good beating, not just by Aunt Jane, but from life itself. She slowly walked over to the dresser and grabbed the towel. She walked towards Jane and eased the gun from her hand.

"If we do this, what would make us different from him? I'm not going to allow his demons to haunt us. His spirit is already dead and headed to a destination of eternal fire. We couldn't do anything to him any worse than that."

Jane walked back over to the dresser and placed the gun on top. She pulled out a drawer and grabbed a navy blue and gold box from it. She handed it to Charlie without saying a word. Charlie thanked her and made her way back to the stairs. She looked back at her aunt who seemed disappointed yet understanding of Charlie's decision. There seemed to be an unspoken language between the two ladies. They both had to learn to deal with this devastating development. The obvious difference was that her aunt had to literally live with it. Charlie wasn't sure what her aunt was ultimately going to do. She had no desire whatsoever to stick around and see either. Charlie got in the car and didn't bother looking back.

The next couple of days were depressing for Charlie. She had decided that she wasn't going to tell Jodie or Joey what Aunt Jane had discovered. She knew it would be too much for Jodie's sensitive nerves and Joey would probably go and kill Jerry on the spot.

As Charlie sat alone on her sofa being comforted by Mechè, she couldn't fathom how this man could stay around them knowing what he had done to their mother, or allegedly done. Her thoughts plagued her with what her mother's last words may have been. *Did she beg for her life or was it an instantaneous death? Did he sneak up on her like a thief in the night or was she aware that it was Jerry?* Perhaps if Jodie hadn't run away when she did, he may have been prone to do something worse to her, too.

Charlie's consistent thoughts and frequent panic attacks had disturbed her peace while causing ongoing nightmares. Her lack of sleep caused her not to be able to fully concentrate on her cases. A part of Charlie regretted ever going on that trip. As much as Aunt Jane claimed to have not known anything, there had to be some indication that Jerry wasn't a sane man. You can't just live with someone that long and they fail to slip up at some point.

Charlie decided to take a few days off to get her mind together since her client's court appearance was a week from now. She considered taking a mini vacation to the beach for some needed relaxation. It was no surprise when Charlie's phone interrupted her thoughts. Even though she was taking time off, people weren't taking time off from her.

"Why do you always make erratic decisions without contacting me?" Joey argued as Charlie answered.

"Joey, I've been very consumed these last few days. I have no idea what you're talking about, so feel free to fill me in on whatever it is that you're complaining about again."

"I'm talking about you calling in a surprise drug test on Reece."

In the madness of everything else, Charlie had forgotten about her retaliation on Reece for sending Winston. She figured she'd get a threatening call from Reece at some point, but she didn't expect Joey to be upset about it. Either way, she still didn't regret what she had done. Reece had it coming.

"Joey, this woman deserved it. Although I do feel she could have been granted a few more hours with her son, she absolutely doesn't deserve another joint custody hearing. Perhaps this new development will help get her life back on track for my nephew."

"It's not your position to decide when she gets help, Charlie. This woman has been calling and threatening my housekeepers. She's telling the police that I got drugs in the house and some mo shit. We had just started back getting to a point where our communication was getting better."

"She's just a little upset, but she'll get over it. She's a loose cannon and she does things without thinking about the consequences. She has got to learn not to send people to my job or endanger my sister. You two both know that I do not play about my family, so I'm having a hard time understanding why you seem so aggravated. Besides, if you don't have anything in the house, then you don't have anything to worry about."

"That's not the point, Charlie. You're not calling in favors solely on my behalf; you're doing shit because you have a personal vendetta with Reece."

"You're damn skippy I have a personal vendetta with her. I checked out Winston's file and he rolls with some very serious people."

"Listen, I know all about this Winston character. Jodie already told me about this dude, and I got that shit handled. I worked something out through some mutual acquaintances, so he is gone for good. I told Jodie no more fuck shit, and she needs to focus on her unborn child. I also want you to find someone to add a little more finesse to your life. Perhaps you wouldn't be so quick to abuse the legal pull that you have."

"You weren't saying anything about my pulls when I was getting cases tossed out for you and your home boys, now were you?"

"Charlie, must we always go back and forth about this same bullshit. We've both done things for each other. There comes a time when it is time to make a change. I want to do better for my son and his future. So with this being said, I need you to see if you can get those results sponged from her records."

"What? I'm not doing that."

"You have to, Charlie. I want to give her another chance at this family thing."

"Are you fucking insane, Joey? Are you actually thinking of giving her another chance after all she has done?"

"No offense, Charlie, but this is something that you wouldn't understand."

"You're damn right I don't understand. Royce doesn't need this type of instability in his life."

"I'm tired of you thinking that you know what's best for me and my son like I'm your kid or he's your son. I love you, Charlie, but those days are over. Please have the results removed for me, okay?"

Charlie reluctantly agreed to it even though she knew it was a terrible idea. If they got back together, Reece would make sure that she and Jodie would never see Royce, not to mention their constant fighting in front of Royce. Reece also knew that behind Joey, Charlie was powerless. All Charlie knew was that he better not cry to her when shit goes left.

Charlie had fallen asleep that night and had a dream about Joey. They were out on a boat fishing when Joey fell in the water. He reached out his hand, but Charlie couldn't grab it. She watched her brother as he helplessly sank.

Charlie woke up with sweat dripping down her forehead and chest. She walked to the bathroom and wiped her face, recalling the nightmare she just had. She went back and sat down on the edge of her bed. She didn't want to call Joey at two in the morning, but she was worried. Out of all things that could've possibly happened, Charlie's phone rang.

"Charlie, I know it's late. I'm sure you were sleep, but...uh...I thought you...I wanted you to-," Aunt Jane stammered and paused.

Charlie held the phone not knowing what to say. For a minute she thought she may be delusional from the sedatives she took before bed. It was almost like she was in a trance.

"I'm...I'm sorry for the damage we've done. There's nothing I can really do or say that could make things right again. I...I never told you kids any of this, but your grandmother was beaten almost daily by my dad when we were kids. He made her have about three miscarriages and there probably would've been more had things not happened the way that they did. It wasn't until I was about four when she met Joanna's dad. Every other night or so, after my dad had gotten too drunk to function, Rose snuck down to the local pub and saw Joanna's dad. They became close, but Joanna's dad was active military. Rose got pregnant with Joanna and eventually ran away from my dad and allowed your mother's dad to call our house a home. Well, my dad found us. I'm not sure if Joanna ever knew since she was a baby at the time, but I saw her dad shoot and kill my dad. I watched Rose and him carry him out to the woods and bury him from my window. Perhaps they assumed I was sleep. I don't know. I thought I understood why they did it, but maybe I didn't. It wasn't long before I resented Joanna and her dad. I rejoiced when they told us he was killed at war. I even resented Rose even though I knew she didn't pull the trigger. The truth was that she knew."

"That's a lot to live with," Charlie finally said after a long pause.

"No matter how hard we tried, Joanna and I couldn't get along. So, when I met Jerry and she hated him, I think that drew me closer to Jerry in a sick way. Your mother told me she had heard around town that he was convicted of aggravated rape a few years before I met him. I confronted Jerry about it, and he called Joanna a liar, so I let it slide. I…I guess I thought he had changed or maybe someone had gotten the story mixed up. I wanted to believe that Jerry was just as good as Joanna's dad was. I was a fool who was fooled by a fool."

There was another awkward moment of silence. Charlie still didn't know what else Aunt Jane was expecting her to say. All this information was so fresh and unexpected. Charlie wasn't able to provide her with any sympathy and she definitely hoped that her aunt didn't expect for her to accept any apologies.

"Anyhow, for what it's worth, I needed you to know I'm taking care of it. I wanted you to know a little history and that I've prayed for God to break any generational curses that linger, so you kids and your kids can have a fulfilled life."

"Thank you, Aunt Jane. I'll pray for us all as well. And we do still love you."

"Thank you, Charlie. I definitely needed to hear that."

Charlie wasn't sure if Aunt Jane wanted to say something else, so she held the phone a little while longer before hanging up. She heard some strange shuffling on Aunt Jane's end and then a weird clicking sound. Right after that, Charlie heard a loud (*Bang!*).

Charlie instantly dropped the phone.

Chapter 13

Charlie was not only baffled by another one of her aunt's daunting confessions, but was angered that her aunt would selfishly leave such a horrific lifelong memory. She had immediately called the police and explained that an emergency crew needed to be sent to her aunt's address as quickly as possible. Charlie didn't want her aunt to die, but she wasn't sure what Aunt Jane was trying to accomplish in that moment. Who fucking shoots themselves just to let someone else hear it? Even though Charlie dealt with drug dealers, cheating spouses, embezzlement, murder, and all other type of criminal cases, it was the most twisted shit that Charlie had ever experienced. Why should she be punished with this appalling recollection in addition to the disturbing past her aunt claimed she had experienced?

It was almost like Aunt Jane was saying that Joanna deserved to die since Grandma Rose helped to conceal Joanna's dad murdering her dad. However, it wasn't okay for Jerry to be the one to kill Joanna and rape her daughter on top of it, so it was her duty to take out an already dying man. It was all too sick and complex. Aunt Jane was making things out to be some unspoken karma. She acted as if she was innocent of everything.

There was no way Aunt Jane was going to make her believe that she knew nothing about Jerry's evil ways. It was probably the reason why she stayed away so much. Then, she had the nerve to slick blame her own mother for her demons. Charlie wasn't sure if she even believed such a horrendous story. It wasn't like anyone else was around to defy her story. If there was any legitimacy to this catastrophe, it was a damn shame that one innocent truth of Jodie being pregnant had uncovered three generations of lies, murder, and deception.

The following day, the investigators had told Charlie that the deaths appeared to be a murder-suicide. Jerry was found dead in the basement on his bed with three gunshots to his chest. The officers said that they found her aunt a few feet away next to a dresser. It was the last place that Charlie had seen her standing before she had left her house the other night, but she dared not to tell the investigators about the visit. When the investigator asked Charlie was she going to be able to come down to talk and maybe collect a few things, she explained that she was only the niece and her aunt had children that could do that. It was yet another surprise to her that her aunt had listed her as the primary emergency contact person. She let the investigators know that her aunt most likely listed her as the emergency contact because she was an attorney, but not her attorney. Charlie also explained that she was contacted by her aunt the night before and she had no idea of the tragedy at hand. She had explained that she wanted nothing to do with the deceased or anything left by the deceased.

Charlie wasn't sure about Joey or Jodie, but she had already decided she wasn't going to the funeral. She wasn't even sure if they were aware of what happened, but it probably didn't matter at this point. Knowing them, they wouldn't show any emotion even if they did feel a type of way. After all Joey had been through from Aunt Jane calling the police on him and Jerry trying to fist fight him when he was only 15, Joey would probably be excited they were gone.

Beyond Joey, the last thing Charlie wanted was for Jodie to feel as if her aunt's suicide was partially her fault since she told their aunt about the abuse. She was also certain that neither of them wanted to run into Aunt Jane's children. No one had seen them since Joey was kicked out of their house. Furthermore, Charlie had also decided that her aunt's version of events would die with her. There was no need in possibly tainting her siblings' image of their grandmother or anyone else for the matter.

*   *   *

About a month had passed and things seemed to be getting back on track. Jodie found out she was having a girl and Santana had proposed to her. Charlie was also excited since this would be her first niece. She had already decided that she was going to spoil her rotten. As she sat at her vanity preparing herself to go to Jodie's engagement party, she received a call from Joey.

"Charlie, I need you. You've got to help me out! Now!" He yelled in panic mode.

"I need you to calm down, Joey. Is Royce okay?"

"Yes, he is fine. This isn't about Royce."

"Okay, so why are you so hysterical?"

"Charlie, I don't want to talk about this over the phone. I need you to get to my house as soon as possible."

"Joey, I can't do that. Jodie is in town and I'm headed out to the engagement party. You are coming, aren't you?"

"Charlie, someone's life is on the line and you're sitting here talking about a damn engagement party. Are you kidding me right now?"

"You said Royce is okay, Jodie is obviously fine, and I'm speaking to you right now. Whose life is in danger?"

"Charlie, could you just come over here?"

"No, you have to be out of your mind. I am not missing my sister's engagement party for another one of your home boy's fuck-ups."

"It's not a home boy, Charlie."

"Okay, well who is it then?"

"I think…I think Reece has been kidnapped."

Charlie held the phone for a minute, not clear if she had heard him correctly. Joey had clearly gone insane. There was no way in hell she was missing her sister's engagement party for Reece Summers. He would have been better off saying that it was his housekeeper or something. She wouldn't miss a damn hair appointment for that tramp, less knowing her sister's party.

"Joey, I'm going to finish getting ready for my real sister's party. I have no interest in Reece or anything that she has going on."

"Charlie, this is not a game. The mother of my child is missing."

"She's probably playing one of her usual games with you and I don't have time for it. Besides, didn't you just tell me to stay out of your personal affairs? Wasn't it you who said I wouldn't understand since I clearly don't have a man?"

"How many times do I have to tell you this is not a damn game? Reece's mother said she found blood on her kitchen floor, the wall, and a business card with Winston Hughes' name on it. He has her!"

"So, you never stopped to think that she could be setting you up or she decided to be with him."

"No, Charlie. She needs our help. Her mother showed me the pictures from her house. This dude wrote COME SEE ME in her own blood on the wall."

"How do you know it's her blood?"

"Huh? He sure in the hell is not about to use his own."

"Why didn't her mother call the police?"

"The card said it would kill her, too, if she got police involved."

"It sounds fishy to me and Reece should have thought about that before she reached out to him. Karma serves her right."

"Charlie, I know you are not that cold-hearted. That is your nephew's mother! You mean to tell me you don't care if she dies?"

"What do you expect me to do, Joey? You want me to go and help you bust down some doors for her? Don't you have muscle for that?"

"I need you to make a few calls, so you can track Winston's cell phone records and Reece's cell phone records. I'm going to head over to her house right now."

"Oh gosh…Joey, I'm on my way right now to meet you at her house."

"No, Charlie. I'm going over there on my own. Besides, this Winston dude may still have it in for you, too."

"Joey, I have metal protection."

"I'm telling you no, Charlie, just make the calls. Please." He said as he ended the call.

Since Joey seemed overly concerned, Charlie was going to meet him anyway but decided against it. What sense did tracking the calls make? Was he trying to prove to her that he was right about Reece? Did he expect for her to have a heart for Reece after she just put all of their lives in danger? She refused to get herself involved with any foolery that Reece had created. Reece was full of drama, so Charlie felt like it was a cry for attention. It was just like the time she claimed she tried to kill herself. The doctor had told Joey that she only swallowed about three or four ibuprofen tablets, which were appropriate milligrams for her to consume. Not only did Charlie take Joey's advice, she decided not to participate at all.

Besides the fact that Charlie hated Reece and was sick of bailing Joey's friends out of shit, he clearly stated that he was tired of her treating him like a kid. It was time for Joey to grow up and handle his own shit. Perhaps letting him take care of something without her would give him a sense of self empowerment and responsibility. In retrospect, perhaps she was actually granting him his last request.

Chapter 14

Charlie arrived at the party about thirty minutes later dressed to
kill. She had on her black red bottoms with a form-fitting, off the
shoulders dress and her natural curly hair was pinned up to
perfection. Although she was already slim, the way her black dress
hugged her hips gave her endless curves. Since Jodie was pregnant,
she was going to be the sexy sister tonight.

As she walked through the corridors, it seemed as if all eyes
were on her. She had recognized quite a few people by association,
but they probably didn't know who she was in this type of attire.
Charlie had an objective and it wasn't just seeing her sister. She
wouldn't admit it to anyone, but she felt some type of way when her
family and associates ragged on her about not having a man. Charlie
had been questioned about her sexual preference on a few occasions.
Even though mostly it was in a joking manner from those closest to
her, she still felt somewhat bothered. Not that it was anyone's

business, but Charlie was actually interested in all types of guys from black, Italian, to Hispanic. She dated an Italian man back in college who she felt she was in love with. When she found out he was married and illegally in America, she secretly reported him, which had eventually gotten him deported. She vowed that it was her first and last time falling in love. Her new Love became her work.

That was many years ago and Charlie was ready to mingle. Although she had never met Santana in person, from the photos and videos that Jodie had sent made it appear as if he ran in good circles. Then there was the fact that Jodie had promised her some eye candy at the party.

She walked over to the VIP section where she spotted Jodie and Santana intimately hugged up with each other.

"Is this my future brother-in-law?"

Charlie said, tapping Santana who had his back turned.

"Charlie!" Jodie yelled, excited to see her sister. "You look incredible!" She continued as she moved pass her fiancé to hug her.

"Thank you, Sweetie. You look amazing as well. You are glowing." Charlie responded, embracing Jodie.

"So, you're the beautiful sister that my angel always brags about. It's definitely a pleasure to be in your presence," Santana said, kissing her hand with his million dollar smile and Latin accent.

"It's a pleasure to finally meet you in person. My sister never looked more beautiful than she does now. Congratulations to you both and thank you for taking good care of her."

"No, thank you and your brother for helping to keep her safe. She is my world and now she's carrying my little princess. No other man could be as happy as I am. I will protect them with my life."

"Aww... I love you, poppy," Jodie said as she rewarded him with a passionate kiss.

Charlie was happy for her sister, but she was also slightly envious. Charlie had been a good girl all these years, motivated, successful, wealthy, but she was still lonely. However, here Jodie was beautifully laced in a baby pink dress and draped in pearls with a gorgeous fiancé on her arm, but had been tricking all of her life and was the ringleader of an escort service just a few moths ago.

"Earth to Charlie. Did you hear me? Is Joey still coming?"

"Uh... I'm not sure."

"Well, did you talk to him?"

"I did. He said he had something to handle."

"Oh, okay." She said and winked.

Jodie probably assumed that Joey was doing a drug deal, so Charlie didn't say anything different. Jodie hated Reece more than she did, so there was no way she was telling her that he was skipping her party for Reece. Hopefully, he would see that the girl was a loony-tune and make it to his sister's party.

"Charlie, I have someone I want you to meet," Santana said, motioning for someone to come over.

"Dominick, this is Charlie. Charlie, this is my best man, Dominick."

All of the negative thoughts about Reece had subsided. This man that stood before her looked like something out of a magazine.

His slender frame complimented his height and his skin had a succulent tan. He had dark wavy hair and a chiseled baby face. He reminded Charlie of a younger looking Mark Consuelos.

"Pleasure to meet you, madam," Dominick said, reaching for Charlie's hand.

The soft kiss that he had placed sent shivers down her spine. His entire demeanor had Charlie intrigued. Although Santana seemed like a good guy, Charlie didn't know anything about his personal life. Hell, she wasn't even sure how much Jodie knew about him. Therefore, she was definitely going to be cautious with this Dominick character no matter how good he looked.

"It's nice to meet you as well, Dominick."

"Jodie brags all the time about her beautiful sister who is an attorney like me."

"Wow! That's interesting. What's your main practice?"

"I practice just about anything you can name. From family disputes to the Nike sign isn't proportionate on my shoes."

Dominick's sense of humor broke the ice and helped Charlie to relax. About an hour later, they found themselves talking at a private table away from the rest of the party. The night seemed magical. Everyone was laughing and enjoying one another's company. It wasn't until a few minutes later that everything changed.

"Charlie! Charlie!" Jodie squealed, unable to catch her breath.

"Jodie, what's wrong, Sweetie? Sit down and breathe," Charlie demanded, hurrying to get to her sister's aid.

"Joey...Joey's been in a shootout," Jodie said, crying in agony.

Chapter 15

"What do you mean Joey's been in a shootout?" Charlie asked.

"One of Joey's people called me and said that they were all in a shootout and Joey was hit," Jodie tried to explain, still out of breath.

"Well, where is he?"

"I don't know. It sounded like the guy that called was struggling himself. He could have been Joey's friend, Andy or Paul. I'm not sure."

Charlie immediately called Joey with no success of him answering. She stopped to collect her thoughts and considered the possibilities of where he may have been. She knew he likely went to find Reece, but was he still at her house? The last thing she wanted to do was call Reece, but she was out of options. While she was considering calling Reece, the hospital called her.

"Yes, is this Ms. Charlie Johnson?" The nurse asked.

"Yes ma'am."

"We have your brother Joey Johnson here in ICU. We intend on performing an emergency operation and we need you to sign some paperwork."

Charlie knew they weren't going to answer any questions over the phone, so she didn't bother asking. After receiving further instructions from the nurse, Charlie borrowed Jodie's flats and immediately headed to the hospital. Her heart was racing as she began to overwhelm herself with thoughts of Joey's condition. She couldn't imagine life without her little brother. She had promised Grandma Rose that she would take care of him. She had always managed to fix his mistakes. This time was different. Charlie was helpless. This wasn't something she could patch up and make it work. All she could do was stand by, watch, and pray.

Charlie had never been as nervous and fidgety in her life than she was when she walked up to the nurse's station. After signing in as Joey's legal guardian, she sat down and waited for the doctor. Jodie had sent her a message, promising to be there as soon as she could.

Sitting down by her lonesome for half an hour gave Charlie that much more time to think and start blaming herself. If only she had helped Joey when he called like she always did, this wouldn't have happened. The one time that she made him figure out something serious for himself caused a tragic outcome. How could this have happened? The more she thought about it, her sadness turned to rage. Reece had to have done this! Charlie warned Joey that she was wicked, but Reece had another thing coming if she thought she was getting away with this. She got up, grabbed her phone from her purse, and walked outside the front door. Charlie began to call every home boy that she had represented on Joey's behalf. Her first two calls were unsuccessful, but she finally reached one of Joey's friends named James that Charlie had gotten off in a self-defense case.

"What do you mean you're not about that life," Charlie yelled, "If it wasn't for us, your life would be over! If you don't-"

"Charlie, what's going on?" Jodie asked, walking as fast as she could with her baby bump in flip-flops to get to her sister's side.

"This asshole said he's not willing to help me find Reece after I just got him off a twenty-five to life prison sentence. He got me fucked up if he think I'm about to let this shit ride."

"Charlie, please stop. Hang up the phone. This isn't you." Jodie pleaded.

"No! I'm fixing this shit like I should have done in the first place!"

"Charlie."

"Leave me alone, Jodie. This shit is about to get handled."

"Charlie, you're upset and you're hurting. Let's talk, okay?"

"James, can you hear me?" Charlie screamed, ignoring her sister.

"Charlie." Jodie said a little louder.

"Jodie, could you please go and wait for the doctor while I handle my business."

"Charlie, Reece is dead! She's gone!" Jodie finally cried out.

Charlie quickly hung up the phone. She looked at her sister in disbelief. She hated Reece, but she didn't wish death on anyone.

"What?"

"Reece was shot and killed in the crossfire."

Charlie just stood there trying to register what her sister had said. She wanted to say something, but no words would come out of her mouth. Jodie slowly walked closer and gave Charlie a firm yet intimate hug.

They both walked inside and sat down to wait for the doctor. It was almost one in the morning, so there were only a few people sitting in the area. Jodie was already running out of patience after asking a second nurse for any updates regarding Joey's condition. About five minutes later a doctor came out requesting Charlie.

"Hello Ms. Johnson, I'm Doctor Forrester. I'm not sure how much information you have, but Joey was shot three times. The bullet in the upper arm and shoulder didn't cause as much damage as the one lodged in his back. If we remove the bullet that penetrated in his back, he could bleed out instantly. However, if we don't remove it, he could bleed internally which could ultimately have the same result. We've got a specialist flying in as we speak for any and all alternative approaches."

"With all due respect, Dr. Forrester, that's kind of like saying do you prefer a plane wreck or a train wreck."

"Ms. Johnson, I do apologize because I know the information that I am giving you is extreme. However, due to the extent of his injuries the procedures are also going to be extreme. I want you to know that we are taking all the necessary precautions to prevent your brother from succumbing to his injuries."

"Is he conscious?"

"Yes, but we gave him a significant amount of pain medication, so he may be a little loopy. You're more than welcome to go and speak with him."

Charlie didn't fully explain to Jodie what the doctor had told her to prevent her from getting hysterical. She let her know that Joey was stable and resting, so she should go home and rest as well. After walking Jodie to her car, she got her a visitor's pass and went to the ICU to see Joey.

As soon as Charlie opened the door, Joey turned his head toward the sound. He was hooked up to several tubes and monitors, but he didn't look as bad as she had imagined. As she walked over to him, he lifted the oxygen mask that covered his mouth and nose. She could still see his pain through the forced grin that he gave. It took everything in Charlie not to burst into tears.

"You need to stop pretending like you're hurt just so you can see these nurses," Charlie said, trying to suppress her emotions.

"These nurses falling in love with me already," he replied as he tried to chuckle but began to choke.

He briefly placed the mask back on while he got his breathing back in sync. Charlie quickly turned her head as tears rushed down her cheeks. She figured the doctor hadn't told him he was practically dying unless this specialist had a miracle solution. She was also going to refrain from telling him Reece was dead for the time being.

"Go ahead and give it to me straight, sis."

"Joey, you're doing fine. Everything is going to be okay."

"Charlie, I'm hooked up to like five different machines with thirty tubes stuck into my body. You know I know better than that."

"Tell me what happened, Joey."

Joey let out a long sigh as his eyes rolled toward the ceiling. He was quiet for a minute and then a tear rolled down the side of his face.

This was the first time that Charlie had remembered seeing Joey cry.

"I went to Reece's house. All the lights were out accept for the one in the kitchen. I had already told Paul and Andy to go around the back and make sure it was all good. When I walked toward the kitchen island, there were papers on the table for me to give up my rights to Royce. I heard a man's voice telling me to sign them or I die. I knew then this was some shit Reece had paid someone to do. The dude was hiding somewhere because I couldn't see anyone. I started yelling; calling Reece bitches and hoes because I knew she was there. I told the nigga I'd rather die than give up my rights. That's when I felt three hot stings in my body. I dropped to the floor, but I heard at least six or seven more shots. Paul eventually came over and lifted me up to see if I was still alive. He turned on the hallway light and pulled off the dude's ski-mask. It was...it was Reece. She was lying on the floor in a pool of blood beside a voice recorder and a gun. She set up the whole fucking thing on her own."

Charlie was speechless. She had her reservations about Reece, but she wouldn't have even once thought of her as being a killer.

"I know what you're thinking. You're thinking how you told my ass that she was a phony and I said to mind your own damn business. You even asked me was it a setup. I was so fucking dumb and blinded by a fantasy that I didn't...," Joey paused and closed his eyes.

Charlie could tell the medication was wearing him down. She refused to add insult to injury by agreeing with him. She held his hand as he continued to fight his fatigue.

"I needed you to be wrong for once. So, I decided to show you I was right. And as wrong as I was, I was finally right for once, Charlie. Had you come with me, I'm certain Reece would have tried to kill you."

Charlie hadn't thought about it. Perhaps she was the target the entire time. Everyone knew that Charlie and Joey were figuratively joined at the hip. So, since Reece couldn't get Charlie, she got Joey instead.

"Grandma had whispered to me once." Joey continued. "She said to always forgive Jodie, follow Charlie, but fight to become the leader. How could she predict that Jodie would run away? How did she know that you would be a lawyer? How? We were still kids."

"Grandma Rose's protection is spiritually infinite. You are a true survivor, Joey. And that's what makes you the leader."

"Do you think I'll see them when I get there?"

"We'll all reunite when it's our time." Charlie answered, holding back more tears.

Joey smiled and closed his eyes, dozing off in a peaceful slumber. Charlie said a prayer as she placed a kiss on his forehead.

"Rest now, little brother."

A week later, Charlie had gone to meet up with Jodie at the grave site. It was something that neither of them had expected to do. With all that had happened, it was just a matter of time. It took everything in Charlie not to reverse her car and leave. She hadn't done this since she was a kid, but her only choice was to pay her respect. She knew no matter if she ran away now or later, life was something that she couldn't reverse or run away from. She stopped and parked her car as she took off her shades. She took a deep breath and talked herself out of the car.

Charlie walked over to Jodie who was already standing beside the grave. She gave her a consoling hug and stepped back in silence. They both stared at the grave, not knowing what to say. All of a sudden a warm breeze settled between their flowing locks of hair. They knew that Grandma Rose was present as well.

"I didn't think we'd be back here anytime soon," Jodie admitted, rubbing her belly.

"We wanted you to know that we love and miss you. We know you're probably up there with momma, so give her a kiss for us." Charlie added.

"When I was a child, I spoke as a child, I understood as a child, I thought as a child; but when I became a man, I put away childish things. Thank you, grandma, for showing us the way." Joey said as he rolled up in his wheelchair.

The Author

Thank you for taking the time to read "We Were Still Kids" by Nataisha T Hill.

"I look forward to providing you with future entertainment that you will enjoy."

Feel free to also enjoy other books and guides that are also available on popular online retailers.

Thank you for your purchase! Here are some additional books by the author.

Guides
Unleashing Essential Oils: With Extra Invaluable Beauty Tips

E-book Supplier for First Time Home Buyer

My Diet Your Diet Our Diet

Experience of Life vs. Expert Advice

Children Book
Little Cupcake's First Day

Novels and Novellas
Partially Broken Never Destroyed I, II, III, IV, V, VI

Alyce Leaves Wonderland

Short Stories
After Dawn Breaks

A Crime for Two

The Doctor's Inn: A Private Practice

Made in the USA
Coppell, TX
14 November 2020